This Orchard
book belongs to

_____

_____

_____

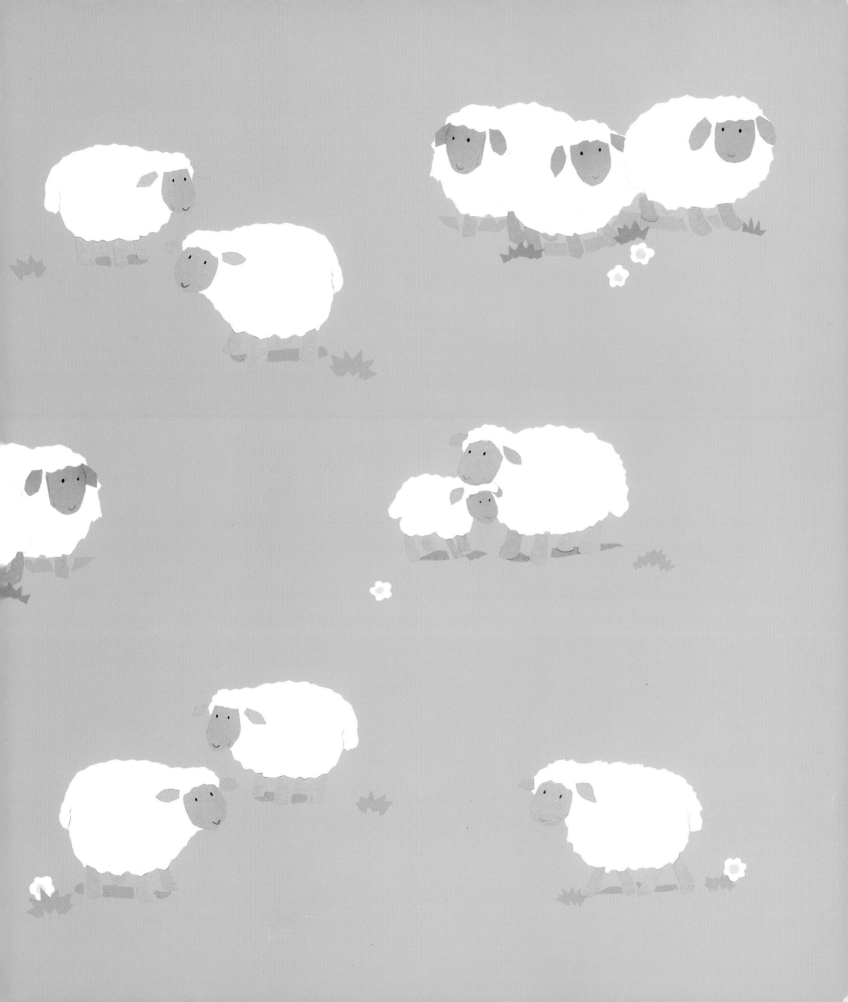

Faraway Farm

For Ella Rose Kennedy and Teddy Traynor
I.W.

For Holly
A.A.

ORCHARD BOOKS
338 Euston Road, London NW1 3BH
Orchard Books Australia
Level 17/207 Kent Street, Sydney, NSW 2000

First published in 2005 by Orchard Books
First published in paperback in 2005
This edition published in 2006

Text © Ian Whybrow 2005
Illustrations © Alex Ayliffe 2005

The rights of Ian Whybrow to be identified as the author and
Alex Ayliffe to be identified as the illustrator of this work have been
asserted by them in accordance with the Copyright, Designs and Patents Act, 1988.
A CIP catalogue record for this book is available from the British Library.

ISBN 978 1 84362 942 9

3 5 7 9 10 8 6 4

Printed in Singapore

Orchard Books is a division of Hachette Children's Books,
an Hachette Livre UK company.
www.hachettelivre.co.uk

Faraway Farm

Ian Whybrow
Illustrated by Alex Ayliffe

ORCHARD BOOKS

Faraway Farm lies over the hill.

Show me the house and the barn and the mill.

Into the kitchen comes Farmer Flat.

Where's his mug and his dog and his little black cat?

Breakfast!
The children all want to be fed!

Find me some eggs and some milk and some bread.

Time to get ready for milking now.

Where's the stool and the pail and the pretty brown cow?

Farmer Flat's wife has a peep in the sty.

She hears an "OINK! OINK!" – so what does she spy?

Here comes the tractor, the dogs run behind.

What other creatures and birds can you find?

Over the hill,
where the meadow is steep . . .

show me the rabbit and the lamb
and some sheep.

Here comes the wagon,
all loaded with hay.

Who's in there riding, all done for the day?

Hold out some apples
and quietly stand.

Who'll come and eat them from out of your hand?

Everyone's tired, so out goes the light.

Who can we find to say, "Good night! Sleep tight!"

If you enjoyed all the fun-filled pictures in Faraway Farm, why not try another action-packed book from the same illustrator?

1 84121 080 3

£5.99

Dig Dig Digging

Margaret Mayo Alex Ayliffe

"Wonderfully bright, with a bouncily rhythmic text which young mechanics will love – and soon learn off by heart."
THE SCOTTISH BOOK TRUST

Also available in board book!

"... a busy, colourful book full of drama and adventure."
DAILY MAIL

Also available in board book!

1 84121 272 5

£5.99

EMERGENCY!

Margaret Mayo Alex Ayliffe

1 84362 438 9

£5.99

CHOO CHOO clickety-clack!

249

Margaret Mayo Alex Ayliffe

"... the illustrations are vibrant ..."
THE BOOKSELLER BUYER'S GUIDE

Orchard paperbacks are available from all good bookshops, or can be ordered direct from the publisher:
Orchard Books, PO BOX 29, Douglas IM99 1BQ
Credit card orders please telephone: 01624 836000 or fax: 01624 837033.
Visit our Internet site: www.wattspub.co.uk or e-mail: bookshop@enterprise.net for details. To order please quote title, author and ISBN and your full name and address. Cheques and postal orders should be made payable to 'Bookpost plc'.
Postage and packing is FREE within the UK (overseas customers should add £1.00 per book).
Prices and availability are subject to change.